FOR VIVIENNE AND OLIVIA

Text and illustrations copyright © 2007 by Johan Olander

Marshall Cavendish Corporation, 99 White Plains Road, Tarrytown, NY 10591
www.marshallcavendish.us/kids

Library of Congress Cataloging-in-Publication Data
Olander, Johan.
A field guide to monsters : googly-eyed wart floppers, shadow-casters, toe-eaters,
and other creatures / observations and illustrations by world-famous monstrologist
Johan Olander. — 1st ed.
p. cm.
Summary: Reports the habitat, diet, lifecycle, and other characteristics of a variety
of unusual monsters, as observed and recorded by a monstrologist.
ISBN 978-0-7614-5359-8
1. Monsters—Fiction. 2. Imaginary creatures—Fiction. I. Title.
PZ7.O4233Fie 2007
Fic—dc22
2007002274

The text of this book is set in Gorey.
The illustrations are rendered in ink, pencil, watercolor, and oil paint on
various papers and boards. Color additions and enhancements
created with Adobe Photoshop.
Book design by Kristen Branch / Michael Nelson Design
Editor: Marilyn Mark

Printed in China
First edition
3 5 6 4 2

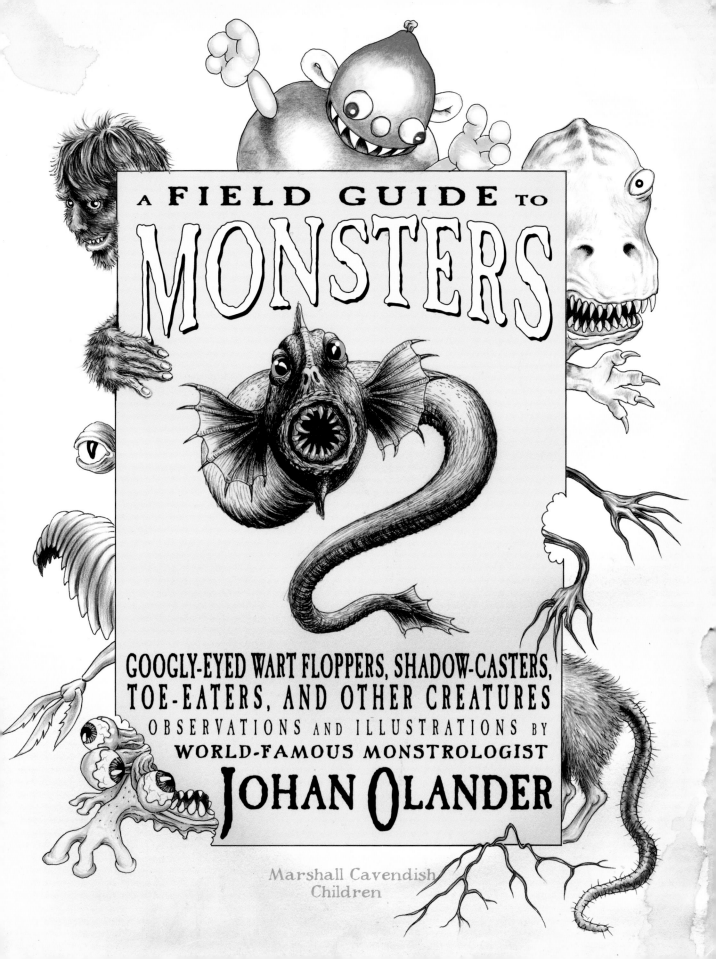

A FIELD GUIDE TO MONSTERS

GOOGLY-EYED WART FLOPPERS, SHADOW-CASTERS,
TOE-EATERS, AND OTHER CREATURES
OBSERVATIONS AND ILLUSTRATIONS BY
WORLD-FAMOUS MONSTROLOGIST
JOHAN OLANDER

Marshall Cavendish
Children

THE MONSTERS

As a monstrologist, I am often called upon by people who claim to have seen mysterious creatures. The monsters depicted in this book include those that I have encountered or those with whom I've had close calls. Other monstrologists might have different research on these monsters or know of other beings not shown here. There are also monsters that you might already be aware of, including werewolves, goblins, and chupacabras, which have a long, well-documented cultural tradition. But as I have no personal experience with this category of creatures, you will not find them in this collection.

Monsters fall into a very subjective area of research. It is possible that there is no single truth. Personally, I believe that there are more monsters in the world than we think.

A BRIEF INTRODUCTION to THE SCIENCE of MONSTROLOGY

The science of monstrology builds on the ancient tradition of observing monsters. Strange beings have always lurked amongst us, though not everyone has had the ability to see them. Children, however, are especially skilled at observing monsters. As we age, it becomes harder to see these creatures, even at close range. This is because monsters inhabit a special space between reality as we know it and the world of fantasy. To see a monster, a person must possess these key traits:

- an open mind
- a keen eye for observation
- a vivid imagination

Thus, some people never see monsters, while others see them all the time. It has become the task of a select few to observe their comings and goings. To be a successful monstrologist, you must cultivate the traits listed above throughout your life.

THE MONSTER HUNT

Tools of the trade that are helpful on a monster hunt include:

- notebook and pencils (Don't forget a sharpener. I did once and lost the chance to sketch a Flesh-Eating Tub Frog.)
- flashlight (Bring extra batteries!)
- old blanket or sheet
- potpourri, cloves, or other strong-smelling items

In the field, the monstrologist sometimes has to hide under a blanket or sheet for long periods of time. It helps if you cut holes for your eyes, so that you can see out while remaining covered. (This is why I recommend an old sheet. Non-monstrologists in your house won't appreciate your cutting up a new one.) A flashlight becomes helpful when making your initial field notes and/or sketching your observations, since it tends to be dark under a blanket. Many monsters have a sensitive sense of smell; cloves or potpourri can be used to mask your human scent, which might otherwise frighten away the monsters (or bring them a little too close).

So, sharpen your pencils, turn on your flashlights, open your minds, and step into the world of monsters!

HAPPY HUNTING!
— Johan Olander

BALLOONSTER

LATIN NAME	*Bulla inflatus*
HABITAT	This monster inhabits balloons of all kinds. It is most often encountered on special occasions and at places such as birthday parties, fairgrounds, and car dealerships.
DIET	A Balloonster consumes gas of any kind—even plain air will do. It does not technically eat; it just gathers gas to grow.

DISTINGUISHING FEATURES	Scientists believe the Balloonster normally exists in gas form and becomes visible only when it inflates balloons. The monster has the ability to create a body or a face out of the balloon it inhabits.
	
	    The Balloonster is not aggressive or dangerous but might startle a human, since it tends to pop. It is always searching for more gas. Plus, the utter absurdity of a large balloon-being is frightening to many people.
	
	    When the Balloonster feels threatened, it can disappear or radically diminish in size in a matter of seconds by letting off gas with a flatulent sound (see drawing on next page).
	
	    It is weightless.

LIFE CYCLE	Balloonsters' life spans vary widely. Some last only a few seconds before encountering their natural enemies (twigs, pins, lightbulbs, fingernails, etc.), while others last for weeks before slowly deflating. Balloonsters have been seen floating in the sky, and their fate remains unknown.
SAFETY MEASURES	Not applicable.

THIS ETCHING BY THE ARTIST JEAN PAUL AULANDRE DEPICTS THE MOST FAMOUS BALLOONSTER APPEARANCE IN HISTORY. IN 1783 THIS BALLOONSTER INHABITED A HOT-AIR BALLOON AND SWOOPED DOWN OVER THE CITY OF PARIS. WITH AN EXTRAORDINARILY LOUD FART SOUND, IT DISAPPEARED. THE BASKET THEN CRASHED ONTO THE ROOF OF THE LOUVRE. THE EPISODE LED TO MASS HYSTERIA, BUT NOBODY WAS SERIOUSLY INJURED. PARISIANS ARE STILL SAID TO BE AFRAID OF LARGE BALLOONS.

THESE BALLOONSTERS DISTURBED MIGUEL ORTEGA'S TENTH BIRTHDAY PARTY IN CLEVELAND, 2006. THEY WERE INADVERTENTLY CREATED BY THE LOCAL CLOWN, SQUEEKY BOO, WHILE HE WAS MAKING BALLOON ANIMALS. LUCKILY A PORTRAIT ARTIST, THE GREAT PICTASSO, WAS IN ATTENDANCE AND WAS ABLE TO MAKE THESE DETAILED STUDIES OF THE BEINGS.

served at: Iowa State Fair 1997

FLEW APPROX. 4 YRDS AND DISAPPEARED

A FLATULENT SOUND EMITTED

ABSOLUTELY NO TRACE OF IT AFTERWARD!

I DREW THIS AFTER SPOTTING A BALLOONSTER AT THE IOWA STATE FAIR IN 1997. AS MY NOTES INDICATE, IT BLEW AWAY WITH A FARTING SOUND, AND THEN ALL TRACES OF IT WERE GONE.

BEACH KRILL

DANGER TO HUMANS

LATIN NAME	*Euphausia litoris*
HABITAT	Beach Krill live by sandy beaches and in and around warm, shallow water.
DIET	The Krill eats human flesh, pets, seagulls, and fish.
DISTINGUISHING FEATURES	A fully grown Beach Krill can be up to 12 feet tall and can weigh up to 200 pounds.

The Krill spends long hours buried under sand or floating near the shore with only its telescopic eyes above the surface. It doesn't like large crowds and is never seen on a beach where there is a lot of activity.

The Beach Krill is sneaky and stays covered until it can snatch a lone beachgoer, swimmer, dog, or seagull without being noticed. A sign of the monster's presence is the strong smell of rotten fish that comes from the monster's always abundant, stinky drool.

BEACH KRILL EGGS. TRUE SIZE IS APPROXIMATELY 3 INCHES IN DIAMETER.

LIFE CYCLE	Krill are born in clusters of transparent eggs the size of tennis balls, which are laid during springtime in shallow waters. The Beach Krill reaches adult size at the end of its first summer and is assumed to spend the winter in the ocean. It has a short life span; the norm appears to be two years.
SAFETY MEASURES	Never swim alone or stray far from your friends.

THIS IS THE CLOSEST I EVER CAME TO A BEACH KRILL ATTACK. I SPOTTED ITS TELESCOPIC EYES PROTRUDING FROM THE SAND WHILE I WAS BUSY WITH A CONSTRUCTION PROJECT (INVOLVING A SHOVEL AND PAIL). UPON CLOSER INVESTIGATION IT DISAPPEARED, LEAVING A HOLLOW IN THE SAND DUNE. I THEN THEORIZED THAT THE KRILL MUST TUNNEL UNDER THE SAND, THOUGH I HAVE HEARD NO OTHER REPORTS OF SUCH BEHAVIOR.

I THINK THIS WAS A GIANT KRILL IT DISAPPEARED WHEN I TRIED TO GET CLOSER...

JUNE 19 -97

THIS MAP FRAGMENT WAS FOUND IN AMSTERDAM IN 1932. IT ONCE BELONGED TO A DUTCH SEA CAPTAIN WHO WAS INVOLVED IN THE SPICE TRADE IN THE 17TH CENTURY. THE MAP DEPICTS A BEACH KRILL GUARDING A TREASURE CHEST. AS THE KRILL WAS FEARED BY SAILORS OF THE 16TH AND 17TH CENTURIES, ITS DEPICTION ON THE MAP WOULD HAVE SERVED AS A WARNING THAT THE LAND WAS INFESTED WITH BEACH KRILL.

BEDWOLF

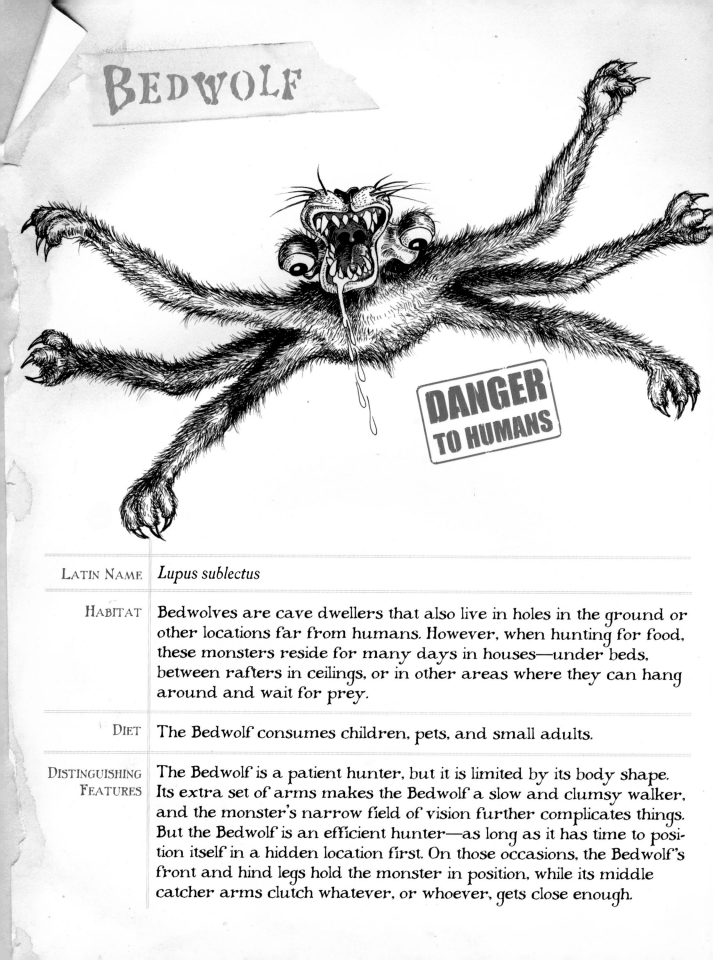

DANGER TO HUMANS

LATIN NAME	*Lupus sublectus*
HABITAT	Bedwolves are cave dwellers that also live in holes in the ground or other locations far from humans. However, when hunting for food, these monsters reside for many days in houses—under beds, between rafters in ceilings, or in other areas where they can hang around and wait for prey.
DIET	The Bedwolf consumes children, pets, and small adults.
DISTINGUISHING FEATURES	The Bedwolf is a patient hunter, but it is limited by its body shape. Its extra set of arms makes the Bedwolf a slow and clumsy walker, and the monster's narrow field of vision further complicates things. But the Bedwolf is an efficient hunter—as long as it has time to position itself in a hidden location first. On those occasions, the Bedwolf's front and hind legs hold the monster in position, while its middle catcher arms clutch whatever, or whoever, gets close enough.

LIFE CYCLE	Young Bedwolf cubs are rarely seen. Bedwolves breed far away from humans, so nothing is known about how they grow up or grow old. It's a subject worthy of more research.
SAFETY MEASURES	If you suspect that you have a Bedwolf under your bed, it is safest to jump into bed rather than climb in—so you never get close to its grasp.

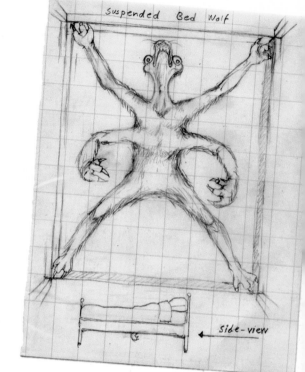

VIEW FROM ABOVE

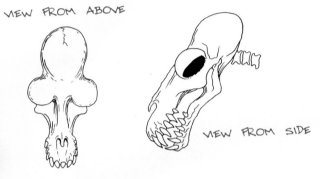

VIEW FROM SIDE

THE CRANIUM OF THE BEDWOLF

It is, in fact, impossible for the monster to look up.

When moving from its hunting areas to its hiding places, the Bedwolf is made vulnerable by this limited field of vision.

THIS THEORETICAL DRAWING SHOWS HOW A BEDWOLF SUSPENDS ITSELF UNDER A BED. I MADE IT AFTER WITNESSING THE CLAW MARKS FROM A BEDWOLF LEFT BEHIND ON A BED FRAME AT MY FRIEND ANGELA'S HOUSE. ANGELA CLAIMED TO HAVE CHASED THE BEAST OFF WITH A BASEBALL BAT. WHEN ASKED TO DESCRIBE IT, SHE SAID, "HE WAS ALL HANDS."

THIS DESIGN CAME FROM A BLANKET WOVEN BY THE ANCIENT AZOOCOTAC TRIBE THAT USED TO INHABIT PARTS OF NORTHERN MEXICO AND THE SOUTHWESTERN UNITED STATES. ANTHROPOLOGISTS STUDYING THIS TRIBE SAY THAT THE BLANKET WAS THOUGHT TO HAVE PROTECTIVE PROPERTIES AGAINST BEDWOLF ATTACKS.

BRUTE

DANGER TO HUMANS

LATIN NAME	*Brutus spiritus*
HABITAT	This monster lives inside humans. Thus, the Brute is really a spirit that inhabits people, causing them to morph into hideous forms. It is usually seen in areas where businesses are open at night.
DIET	The Brute consumes positive human feelings and replaces them with feelings of anger and resentment. The more negative feelings it generates, the more energy it seems to get.
DISTINGUISHING FEATURES	Each Brute looks different—depending on its victim. Brutes warp the features of their victims' bodies. The most telling signs that a human is infected by a Brute are: • a fiery gaze • pulsating temples • clenching jaws • vicious outbursts When humans become infected, they get extremely angry for no good reason.

LIFE CYCLE	The Brute seems capable of dividing itself endlessly into multiple Brutes. Sometimes whole segments of a population become infected, and those large groups can become violent. I, for one, am convinced that World War I was caused by a massive Brute infection that spread throughout western Europe, breeding mayhem. Because the Brute keeps dividing, it lives forever.
SAFETY MEASURES	The only defense against a Brute is to stay as far away as possible from its victims. It is rare for a Brute to stay in a human for longer than an hour at a time, but recurrences are common.

THIS SCHEMATIC DRAWING DEMONSTRATES HOW A BRUTE SPIRIT REPLACES ALMOST ALL POSITIVE ENERGY IN A HUMAN, TRANSFORMING HIS OR HER BEHAVIOR. BRUTES INFECT HUMANS OF BOTH SEXES AND OF ALL AGES, BEGINNING WITH TWO YEAR OLDS (HENCE THE "TERRIBLE TWOS").

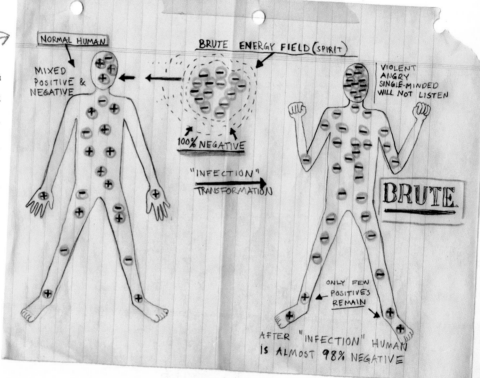

THESE ARE TWO EXAMPLES OF PERFECTLY NORMAL, HEALTHY HUMANS BEFORE AND AFTER A BRUTE INFECTION HAS SET IN.

COMMON
HAIRY BEAST

LATIN NAME	*Bellua pilosus*
HABITAT	The Common Hairy Beast resides in forests and brushland near human dwellings. It is often spotted just outside gardens or in darker, quieter areas of backyards.
DIET	This monster eats snack packs, sandwiches (especially peanut butter and jelly), fruit, and candy.
DISTINGUISHING FEATURES	The Beast's silky, shiny fur and friendly appearance attract children and pets, much like a soft, cuddly teddy bear does.

Children adore this monster, who is sociable and possesses basic language skills. The Beast, however, doesn't trust adults and tends to hide from them.

It has an insatiable appetite and will devour sweet treats in a matter of seconds. The Beast constantly looks for food and always asks the children it befriends to bring more treats.

The adult Common Hairy Beast can grow to be 7 feet tall and can weigh up to 400 pounds.

The Beast also makes a distinctive humming sound when it's hungry. It sounds like this: *Hmm di dum-dum, hmm di dum-dum, hmm di dum-dum.*

LIFE CYCLE	Like many mammals, a Beast mother takes care of her young for the first two years, until the cubs are fully grown but still "teenagers." After that, she pushes them away and encourages them to take care of themselves. Children tend to encounter the Beasts at this time, since the teenage monsters have little life experience, are confused, and are desperate for sweets. They might even accept help from adult humans if no children are around.
SAFETY MEASURES	Not applicable.

The beast has friendly in

THE HAIRY BEAST'S FOOTPRINT IS MUCH LONGER AND THINNER THAN A HUMAN PRINT.

"TEENAGER" HAIRY BEAST

Observed behind Johnstons' Barn Aug. 2004

THIS PAGE WAS TORN OUT OF A 19TH-CENTURY DIARY. IT WAS SENT TO ME FROM AN ANONYMOUS SOURCE AND APPEARS TO SHOW A HAIRY BEAST. THE WORD "FRIENDLY" NEXT TO IT CONFIRMS MY VIEW OF THE BEASTS AS HARMLESS, KIND MONSTERS.

→

THIS YOUNG MONSTER WAS NERVOUS BUT ALLOWED ME TO DRAW ITS PORTRAIT BEFORE IT DISAPPEARED. IN EXCHANGE, I GAVE IT A WHOLE JAR OF STRAWBERRY JAM.

CORNER CAT

DANGER TO HUMANS

LATIN NAME	*Felis angulosa*
HABITAT	Corner Cats typically linger in dark corners, waiting for a chance to attack. Nooks behind open doors are a favorite vantage point. But where this monster actually lives is a mystery.
DIET	This vicious creature eats humans.
DISTINGUISHING FEATURES	The Corner Cat is shy, quick, and quiet. Its lightning-fast sneak attacks result in a small bite on the victim's ankle. The Cat can grow to be about 3 feet tall but is very, very thin. It rarely causes serious harm to adult humans. For children, however, an attack by a Corner Cat can cause grave injuries.
LIFE CYCLE	It is believed that Corner Cats live for a long time and that only a few have existed throughout history. One is rumored to have haunted the pyramids of Egypt for more than three thousand years.
SAFETY MEASURES	Wear rubber galoshes or leather boots that cover your ankles to protect yourself from Corner Cat bites.

This Corner Cat, depicted on papyrus, is a copy of an older wall painting found in the Pyramids of Giza.

The house cat's footprint, left, is quite different from the Corner Cat's, right.

A child named Abdul sent me this from Philadelphia. He found it among his grandfather's old papers. It was in a letter dated 1903, addressed to his grandfather's older brother but never sent. In it, Abdul's grandfather describes his experiences in Egypt and seeing "this strange, catlike being" inside a pyramid. He writes:

"I hesitate to include this drawing as I fear you might think I have completely lost my marbles, but I swear that this is what I saw. I only caught a glimpse of it, as this swift and terrifying beast gave my tour guide a nasty bite above his heel. The man later refused to talk about it and pretended as if nothing had happened, though he walked with a limp."

DARK OOZE

LATIN NAME	*Mucus malus*
HABITAT	Dark Oozes dwell in or near water: rivers, lakes, ponds, and even puddles.
DIET	The Dark Ooze does not eat in the way animals or humans do. Instead it just absorbs material and grows into the size of what it has consumed. It only absorbs things with a high liquid content, such as human or animal bodies, fruit, sewage, and chemical waste. Nothing comes out of the Ooze; once absorbed, all is lost.
DISTINGUISHING FEATURES	This shapeless monster can evaporate, melt, or become liquid at will. When it is in a semisolid state, as in the image above, its rotten smell attracts flies, which will hover above it. Likewise, Dark Ooze is attracted to strong odors. Few have lived to tell the tale, but it is said that if you come in contact with the Ooze, it feels like touching runny, ice-cold Jell-O. The monster is especially frightening when it wells up in a "standing" position, ready to engulf you. As the Ooze moves on dry land, it glides forward with a sound similar to the last slurps of a milkshake. The size and weight of an Ooze are virtually limitless.

LIFE CYCLE	Some theorize that there might, in fact, be only one Ooze in the world and that all smaller Oozes are actually one being. All we know is that at the core of every Ooze, there is a pair of eyes and a bundle of "nerves" with some type of "nodes" that perhaps act as part of a central brain.
SAFETY MEASURES	The best human defense against this monster is meticulous hygiene. A clean-smelling human is of no interest to the Ooze.

NODES

NERVES →

THE CORE OF THE OOZE. THE "NERVES" MIGHT BE MUCH LONGER THAN DEPICTED.

THE DRAWING ABOVE WAS FOUND IN THE DIARY OF THE FAMOUS ENGLISH ROMANTIC POET, WILLIAM PHAKE (1767–1839).

ALSO FOUND ON A TORN-UP PIECE OF PAPER STUCK IN THE DIARY WAS THIS POEM (LEFT) DESCRIBING AN ENCOUNTER WITH DARK OOZE:

"THERE IT STANDS BEFORE ME
AN OOZING MASS OF MALICIOUS DARKNESS
FROZEN BY A CHILL SO GLOOMY
I'M HELD FAST IN LIQUID MADNESS"

There it stands before me
An oozing mass of malicious
darkness
Frozen by a chill so gloomy
I'm held fast in liquid madness

DOMESTIC DUST-DEVIL

LATIN NAME	*Sarcinula diaboli domestica*
HABITAT	The Domestic Dust-Devil is common indoors in all parts of the world, especially under furniture and in dark corners. Its favorite habitat is bedrooms.
DIET	This monster consumes primarily dust bunnies, but it eats anything small and light enough to be caught by its barbed "hands"— even smaller Devils. Bread crumbs and other pieces of human food, as well as human hair and plain dirt, are some of its favorite foods.
DISTINGUISHING FEATURES	The Dust-Devil is aggressive and greedy, and it can grow to a surprising size in a short time. Adult individuals usually reach 3 to 4 inches in width, but there have been unconfirmed reports of Dust-Devils as wide as a foot. The limbs of the Dust-Devil's skeleton (see fig. 1 at right) are full of barbs (fig. 2) that firmly catch dust bunnies and other prey. The Dust-Devil weighs only a few ounces and can hover or ride on sudden wind bursts. It does not make any sounds.

LIFE CYCLE	The Dust-Devil has the ability to replicate itself. Once it has grown to a large enough size, its limbs develop into separate individuals. Little else is known about the life cycle of the Dust-Devil. It is presumed that the Dust-Devil lives for no more than a few months, but no firm data exists.
SAFETY MEASURES	Not applicable. However, you may want to note that the Domestic Dust-Devil's natural enemy is the vacuum cleaner.

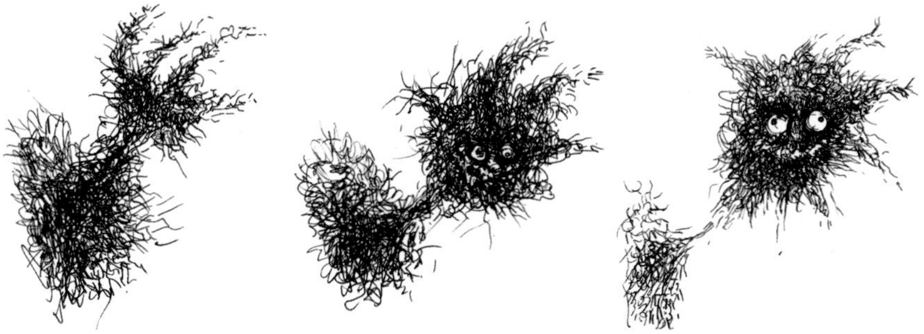

AN ADULT DUST-DEVIL EJECTS ITS OFFSPRING FROM ONE OF ITS LIMBS.

THIS FIELD NOTE IS FROM AN EXPEDITION TO MY GRANDMOTHER'S HOUSE. HER HOUSE IS FILLED WITH OLD FURNITURE AND DRAPERIES, CREATING A PERFECT HABITAT FOR DUST-DEVILS. UNFORTUNATELY FOR THIS DUST-DEVIL, I PERSUADED GRANDMOTHER TO LET ME DO SOME CLEANING UP, AND HE WAS NO MATCH FOR HER HOOVER.

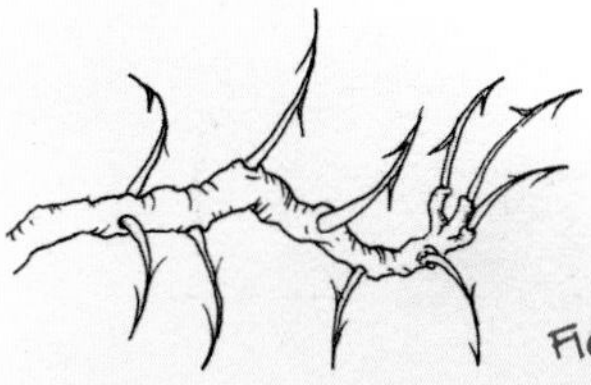

FIG. 1

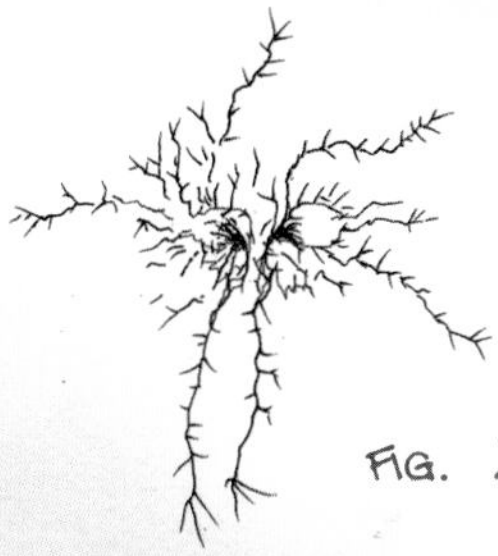

FIG. 2

THE SKELETON, OR FRAME, OF THE DUST-DEVIL IS A BUNCH OF HARDY STRANDS OF FIBER WITH BARBS.

02-27-04
Hunting Dust-Devil
observed under
grandma's bed

Approx. 8" tall

Later this D.D got
Vacuumed by me

DRAINER

LATIN NAME	*Exhaustor quisquiliarum*
HABITAT	The Drainer nests in basements and crawl spaces but can usually be found feeding under the kitchen sink.
DIET	This monster eats anything that comes through the drain.
DISTINGUISHING FEATURES	The Drainer has a unique snout that allows the monster to attach itself to drains on kitchen sinks. It makes a loud growl when something comes down the drain; it sounds like a garbage disposal, so it tends to be mistaken for one. The Drainer's sharp teeth can grind almost anything into a rough paste.

It is a gluttonous monster. It will not stop eating until it fills its entire body cavity.

The Drainer excretes water through vents on the sides of its snout. This can cause flooding and water damage throughout the house, which is often blamed on the dishwasher.

LIFE CYCLE	Once a Drainer has eaten its fill, it withdraws to its nesting area to hibernate and give birth to offspring. Some monstrologists believe that a Drainer can hibernate for several years, sending its children out into the world to grow up completely on their own.
SAFETY MEASURES	Not applicable, though one may wish to call a plumber—the Drainer's worst nightmare.

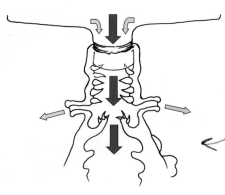

THE DRAINER'S SNOUT IS VERY COMPLICATED AND EFFICIENT. WATER (BLUE ARROWS) IS RELEASED THOUGH TWO VENTS ON THE SIDES OF THE SNOUT. SOLIDS (RED ARROWS) ARE GROUND UP BETWEEN THE MANY TEETH THAT GROW ALL AROUND THE INSIDE OF THE MOUTH.

THIS YOUNG DRAINER WALKED STRAIGHT ACROSS THE KITCHEN FLOOR IN FRONT OF ME DURING A MONSTER-HUNT IN DENVER, COLORADO, 2006. IT HAD A CONFUSED LOOK ON ITS FACE.

UPON SPOTTING ME, IT RETREATED TO THE BASEMENT AND WENT INTO HIDING. I NEVER SAW IT AGAIN.

There was a strange beast under her sink. And it wasn't a plumber, or her husband...

THIS ODD COMIC FRAME WAS SENT TO ME BY A FELLOW MONSTROLOGIST FROM AUSTRALIA AFTER I TOLD HER ABOUT MY ENCOUNTER WITH THE YOUNG DRAINER TO THE LEFT. IT APPEARED IN A LOCAL MAGAZINE THAT CATERS TO THE MONSTROLOGY COMMUNITY.

Eyesore

LATIN NAME	*Vomica ocularia*
HABITAT	Eyesores live in closets and other dark, quiet areas of the house.
DIET	These monsters eat shoes, especially funky-smelling sneakers. Young Eyesores prefer to eat sandals and shoestrings.
DISTINGUISHING FEATURES	The Eyesore is usually encountered when it is feeding, which is inevitably someplace where there are shoes. In general, this creature is not a great danger to humans because of its dietary preference. If the Eyesore is hungry, however, and somebody has been standing still in his or her shoes for too long, the Eyesore will take a bite of the shoe with the foot inside. Luckily, it won't eat the foot.

Because of the great amount of toxins in its body (from devouring smelly shoes), the Eyesore produces a potent poison. It is released through the short, hard bristles on its skin, and contact with the substance causes temporary lunacy in humans and an uncontrollable lust for shoes.

The number of eyes on an Eyesore has little to do with its diet but plays an important part in its child-rearing practices: it always keeps an eye on its only child.

The Eyesore grows to the size of a bulldog and can be equally tenacious.

LIFE CYCLE	The Eyesore raises only one child in its lifetime and is a very caring parent. Eyesores have a long life span (about 80 years), and the child stays with its parent until the parent passes away.
SAFETY MEASURES	Cedar blocks, air fresheners, and shoe deodorant will make your shoes unpalatable to the Eyesore.

THE YOUNG EYESORE IS SURPRISINGLY CUTE.

THIS PRINT BY THE GERMAN EXPRESSIONIST ARTIST PAUL ULF WAS MADE IN 1927. HE PROBABLY TOUCHED THE EYESORE TOO MANY TIMES DURING HIS OBSERVATIONS AS HE WAS INSTITUTIONALIZED IN 1929, AFTER HE BEGAN EATING BOOTS.

THE SHORT, HARD BRISTLES OF THE EYESORE'S SKIN ARE POISONOUS.

FLAPPER

LATIN NAME	*Vespertilio inconcinnus*
HABITAT	Flappers sleep in attics and barn lofts but will roam anywhere to find food.
DIET	Flappers enjoy old, rotten fruit and vegetables.
DISTINGUISHING FEATURES	The Flapper is a clumsy and unwieldy beast that often frightens people unintentionally. For example, the Flapper might try to glide on its flimsy wings through an open window or to a balcony, but it tends to miscalculate speed and distance and crashes. Or, once inside a house, the Flapper might knock down porcelain or other fragile items while stealing some old fruit, thus alerting the whole house to its presence. Its wings are its hands, and despite having a very long life span, it never learns to use them efficiently. A fully grown Flapper can reach 4 feet in height.

LIFE CYCLE	The Flapper lays eggs that resemble peaches in shape and color. Its young grow up alone. This lack of parental guidance seems to be the reason for the monster's poor body control—no role models.
	A normal life span for a Flapper is more than one hundred years, which is remarkable considering the number of bad accidents a Flapper usually experiences during its lifetime.
SAFETY MEASURES	When a Flapper gets cornered, it can bite and scratch, so it is best not to confront one but to give it an easy way to escape.

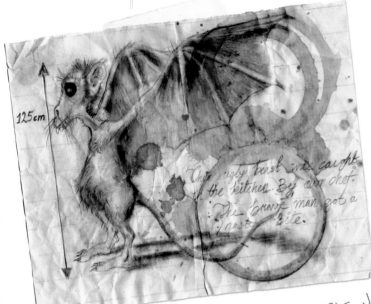

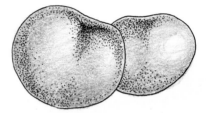

FLAPPERS LAY ODDLY SHAPED EGGS.

THIS IMAGE WAS MADE BY MY GREAT UNCLE JOSEF PAULINUS OLANDER. HE ENCOUNTERED THIS FLAPPER WHILE ON AN EXPEDITION TO CANADA. UNCLE PAULINUS WAS A NOTORIOUS COFFEE DRINKER (HENCE THE STAIN) AND A VERY SKILLED DRAFTSMAN.

THE FLAPPER'S WING/HAND IS AN AWKWARD EXTREMITY. IT APPEARS THAT IT EVOLVED FROM WHAT WAS ONCE A RELATIVELY NORMAL-LOOKING HAND. THE LONG, SLENDER FINGERS HAVE ONLY ONE JOINT AT THE KNUCKLE, SO THIS MONSTER GRASPS OBJECTS WITH DIFFICULTY.

FLESH-EATING TUB FROG

LATIN NAME	*Rana labrum carnivora*
HABITAT	The Flesh-Eating Tub Frog dwells in bathrooms—under tubs and behind toilets.
DIET	This creature eats human flesh, soap, and bath products. It also loves fruit- and bubble gum-scented bubble bath.
DISTINGUISHING FEATURES	Thankfully, this is a rare monster. It can cause a lot of trouble if a bathroom gets infested. If you find one Flesh-Eating Tub Frog, there are often many more.

Tub Frogs grow to about the size of a large frog and seldom pose a mortal danger to humans. The monster's fearsome jaws can manage only a small bite of flesh, but in the same way mosquitoes can drive you insane, a group of Tub Frogs can make your bathroom a very inhospitable place.

The Flesh-Eating Tub Frog makes an ironic, froglike sound as it tears flesh: *rrripp-it, rrripp-it.*

LIFE CYCLE	The Tub Frog's life cycle resembles a normal frog's. After hatching from an egg deposited in standing water—often a sewer—the Tub Frog lives as a tadpole while developing legs and arms. During this stage, the main differences between the Tub Frog tadpole and a regular frog tadpole are the mouth, which already has sharp teeth, and the placement of the eyes, which is higher in Tub Frogs.
SAFETY MEASURES	Keeping a bare minimum of bath products in your bathroom will lessen your chances of having Tub Frogs, since they are attracted to fresh, fruity, flowery smells.

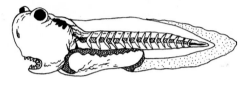

THIS IMAGE WAS FOUND IN A MEDIEVAL BOOK ABOUT HYGIENE. THIS WREATH WAS USED TO KEEP TUB FROGS AWAY.

IT WAS MADE OF THE RARE DUNG BLOOM, A FLOWER KNOWN FOR ITS FOUL ODOR.

THE EYES OF THE TUB FROG TADPOLE ARE PLACED HIGH ON THE HEAD, AND ITS MOUTH IS LINED WITH RAZOR-SHARP TEETH.

WHILE VACATIONING AT MY COUSIN JOHNNY'S SUMMER HOUSE IN MAINE, WE HAD TO USE AN OLD OUTHOUSE FOR OUR TOILET NEEDS, BECAUSE HIS BATHROOM WAS INFESTED WITH TUB FROGS.

I OBSERVED THIS SPECIMEN THROUGH THE BATHROOM WINDOW FOR QUITE A WHILE. IT LOOKED VERY FAT, PERHAPS DUE TO THE FACT THAT JOHNNY SPENDS A TREMENDOUS AMOUNT OF TIME FIXING HIS HAIR (WHICH HE IS LOSING) AND KEEPS AN ARSENAL OF SOAPS AND SHAMPOOS IN THE BATHROOM.

AT COUSIN JOHNNY'S SUMMER HOUSE JUNE 24, 2002

APPROX: 5"

THIS FROG WAS EATING A SOAP-BAR

Googly-Eyed Wart Flopper

LATIN NAME	*Verruca gugelocularis*
HABITAT	Googly-Eyed Wart Floppers live in dark, moist areas both indoors and outdoors. They can be encountered under kitchen sinks and in trash cans and alleys.
DIET	Wart Floppers eat garbage.
DISTINGUISHING FEATURES	The Wart Flopper is an unsanitary but harmless little monster. It enjoys scaring people by jumping out of trash cans or other hiding places and letting out loud burps that stink of garbage. It is believed to transmit warts if you touch its skin, which is covered with hairy warts. Its googly eyes give it almost 360-degree vision and help the monster keep a lookout while hiding and eating. The Googly-Eyed Wart Flopper grows up to 3.5 feet in height and can weigh close to 16 pounds. Its feet make a distinct floppy sound when it walks. In fact, it looks rather humorous as it strolls along, since it walks like a clown wearing oversized shoes.

LIFE CYCLE	Wart Floppers' offspring grow up fast. These monsters can have babies several times a year. If there is an abundance of garbage and good hiding places, large flocks of Wart Floppers can be found—even in small areas.
SAFETY MEASURES	If you see this monster, keep your distance from its warts.

THIS LATE 18TH-CENTURY WATERCOLOR OF A GOOGLY-EYED WART FLOPPER WAS DISCOVERED IN THE STUDY OF A WELL-KNOWN BRITISH NATURALIST IN HIS MANSION IN ENGLAND. HIS FAMILY PREFERS NOT TO DISCLOSE HIS NAME.

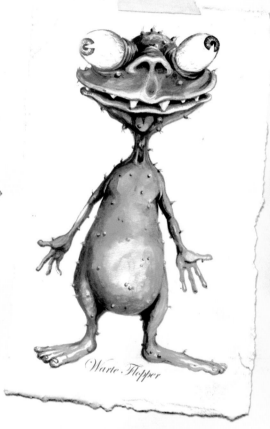

Warte Flopper

I OBSERVED THIS FLOPPER FOR QUITE A WHILE DUE TO MY CLEVER, IF UNFOR-TUNATE, HIDING SPOT: I IMMERSED MYSELF IN A NEIGHBORING GARBAGE CAN IN THIS ALLEY. IT TOOK DAYS TO GET RID OF THE GARBAGE SMELL.

THIS IS WHAT A TYPICAL WART FLOPPER WART LOOKS LIKE UP CLOSE. AS FAR AS I KNOW, THE WARTS SERVE NO OTHER NATURAL FUNCTION THAN TO SPREAD MORE WARTS.

HANGER

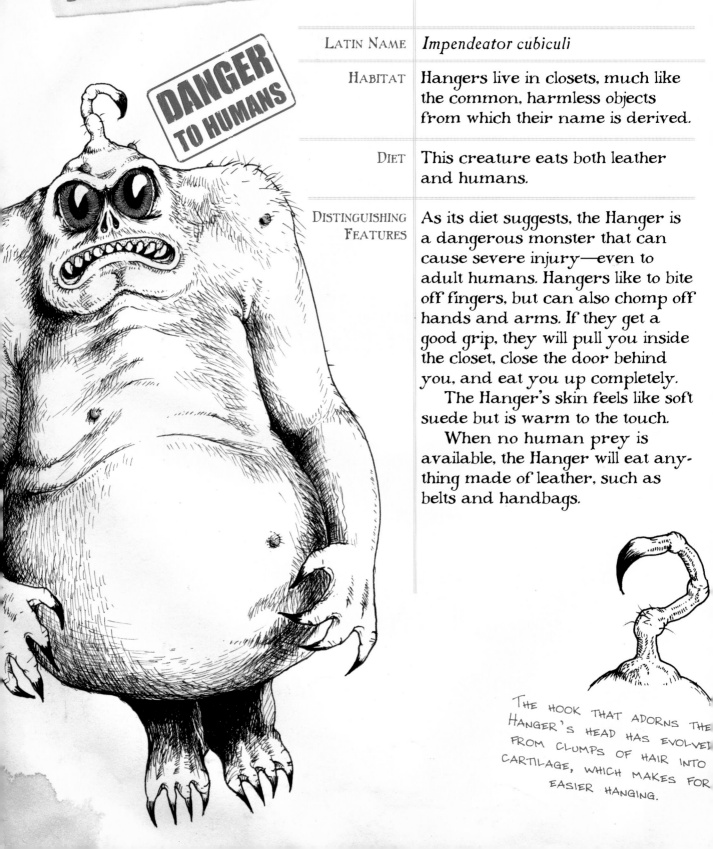

LATIN NAME	*Impendeator cubiculi*
HABITAT	Hangers live in closets, much like the common, harmless objects from which their name is derived.
DIET	This creature eats both leather and humans.
DISTINGUISHING FEATURES	As its diet suggests, the Hanger is a dangerous monster that can cause severe injury—even to adult humans. Hangers like to bite off fingers, but can also chomp off hands and arms. If they get a good grip, they will pull you inside the closet, close the door behind you, and eat you up completely.

DANGER TO HUMANS

The Hanger's skin feels like soft suede but is warm to the touch.

When no human prey is available, the Hanger will eat anything made of leather, such as belts and handbags.

THE HOOK THAT ADORNS THE HANGER'S HEAD HAS EVOLVED FROM CLUMPS OF HAIR INTO CARTILAGE, WHICH MAKES FOR EASIER HANGING.

LIFE CYCLE	Hanger babies are abandoned at birth and must learn to fend for themselves. As babies they are cute and crafty; sometimes they can sneak themselves into a litter of kittens or puppies and survive on milk and pet food until old enough to digest leather. They will never eat pets, since pets are the only family Hangers know.
	Monstrologists are unsure what Hangers do when they're not hunting for leather in our closets.
SAFETY MEASURES	Children should stay far away from closets in which there might be a Hanger. Exercise caution if you've recently lost a leather item inside your closet. This is often the first sign that there's a Hanger in your house.
	Always turn the light on when you are reaching into your closet; the Hanger's large eyes give it excellent night vision, but bright light will blind it.
	Some people have eliminated all leather items in their wardrobes to ward off Hangers. Also, if you trick one into eating something made of fake leather, it will become ill and leave your closet.

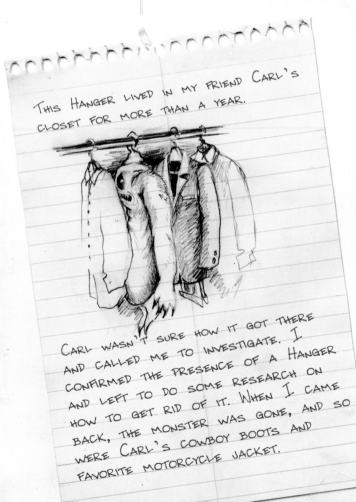

THIS HANGER LIVED IN MY FRIEND CARL'S CLOSET FOR MORE THAN A YEAR.

CARL WASN'T SURE HOW IT GOT THERE AND CALLED ME TO INVESTIGATE. I CONFIRMED THE PRESENCE OF A HANGER AND LEFT TO DO SOME RESEARCH ON HOW TO GET RID OF IT. WHEN I CAME BACK, THE MONSTER WAS GONE, AND SO WERE CARL'S COWBOY BOOTS AND FAVORITE MOTORCYCLE JACKET.

A FEW WEEKS AFTER THE LARGE HANGER LEFT, CARL FOUND THIS BABY IN THE SAME CLOSET, NESTING IN A LOAFER. CARL FED IT MILK AND COOKIES FOR A FEW DAYS, BUT THEN IT BIT HIM AND DISAPPEARED. NOTE: AT THIS AGE THE HOOK ON ITS HEAD WAS SOFT.

JACK

DANGER TO HUMANS

LATIN NAME	*Timor pyxidium*
HABITAT	This monster hides in boxes and other closed-off, dark places.
DIET	Jacks eat children, pets, and occasionally smaller grown-ups.
DISTINGUISHING FEATURES	This monster lives a life unknown to us—until someone opens its box, that is. Once this happens, it jumps out in a flash and catches whomever it can grab. Nobody knows where its victims are taken or where the Jack actually lives. It appears in closed-up boxes and other spaces without any natural way of getting there, and sadly, its victims never return.

The Jack's size can vary greatly, from less than a foot to more than 4 feet in length. Its size seems to have no bearing on what prey it catches. Even larger children or small adults can be taken by a minor Jack. Its arms have an elastic, rubbery quality and can stretch to almost double their normal length.

The only sound the Jack makes is a springy *boing*.

LIFE CYCLE	Unknown.
SAFETY MEASURES	The Jack is afraid of light. If you have empty boxes around the house, always leave them open; the light will prevent Jacks from hiding in them. If you want to open a box that you think might contain a Jack, direct a strong flashlight toward the opening to blind the Jack in case of an attack.

THIS SIDE UP

I OBSERVED THIS FRIGHTENING JACK-ATTACK WHILE ON A HOUSE CALL IN BALTIMORE, MARYLAND, IN 1999. THE FAMILY PET IGUANA HAD MYSTERIOUSLY DISAPPEARED, AND MONSTER ACTIVITY WAS SUSPECTED. THE YOUNG DAUGHTER, FATIMA, WAS ALMOST CAUGHT BY A JACK JUMPING UP FROM A CARDBOARD BOX. IT GOT AWAY WITH ONE OF HER SOCKS.

THE CLASSIC TOY JACK-IN-THE-BOX WAS PROBABLY DEVELOPED AS A TRAINING DEVICE TO HELP CHILDREN PRACTICE AVOIDING JACK-ATTACKS. BECAUSE OF THE RELATIVE RARITY OF ATTACKS, ITS ORIGINAL PURPOSE HAS BEEN FORGOTTEN BY MOST.

LEECH-EEL
A.K.A. TOILET SNAKE

DANGER TO HUMANS

LATIN NAME	*Anguilla hirudo cloacarum*
HABITAT	Leech-Eels live in plumbing fixtures and city sewers. They are often found in toilets (hence the nickname).
DIET	This monster sucks human blood when possible, but gets by on rats most of the time.
DISTINGUISHING FEATURES	Since the Leech-Eel often slithers up from the drains of toilets, it attacks humans "where the sun don't shine" when they are sitting on the toilet seat, thus causing painful and embarrassing injuries. It hunts at night and grows up to 2 feet in length. It can weigh up to 4 pounds. A low, screeching sound, created by the Eel's sharp fin-claws scratching against the porcelain in toilets, is a surefire sign of an impending attack.

LIFE CYCLE	The only thing we know about the life cycle of the Leech-Eel is that the monster transforms from a harmless, fishlike state (see fig. 1 below) when young, to a fearsome beast in adulthood. This transformation is believed to occur during a long migration to the deepest part of the earth's oceans, the Mariana Trench, located south of Japan, where similar creatures have been observed.
SAFETY MEASURES	Turn on the lights in the bathroom at night and slam down the toilet seat a couple of times. The Leech-Eel will then pass by your house and travel through the sewers to prey on some other unfortunate human or find dinner in the form of a sewer rat or two.

FIG. 1

THE BABY LEECH-EEL. AT THIS STAGE IT POSES NO DANGER TO HUMANS.

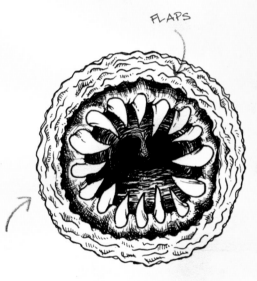

FLAPS

LIPS

THE LEECH-EEL'S MOUTH IS SURROUNDED BY A SOFT LIP WITH MANY SMALL FLAPS THAT HELP IT ATTACH TO A VICTIM LIKE A SUCTION CUP BEFORE IT STARTS TO SUCK BLOOD. INSIDE THE LIPS IS A ROW OF SHARP, VERY CAPABLE TEETH.

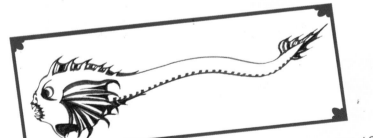

THIS TILE WAS FOUND IN A 13TH-CENTURY ROYAL PALACE IN CHINA AND IS BELIEVED TO DEPICT A LEECH-EEL. IT WAS DISCOVERED IN THE SERVANT'S BATHROOM WITHIN A PLAQUE OVER THE TOILET THAT READ AS TRANSLATED:

"IF THE EMPEROR'S TIME YOU SIT AND WASTE, THE SNAKE BELOW WILL TAKE A TASTE."

MONSTER X

FIG. 1

THIS EGG WAS
FOUND IN A BACK-
YARD IN CONNECTICUT
IN APRIL 2005.

LATIN NAME	*Monstrosaurus rex*
HABITAT	Monster-X resides in garages, barns, garden sheds, and out-buildings.
DIET	This monster is a vegetarian. It eats a lot of fruits, berries, nuts, cookies, candy, and wood.

DISTINGUISHING FEATURES	Monster-X is easily recognized and harmless despite its enormous fanged mouth and large size. A fully grown Monster-X can be up to 24 feet tall. It appears that the monster is attracted to children who don't have many friends. It loves to play with children and has simple language skills. It says things such as, "Me like," "More," "Yum-yum," "No," and "Yes" in its soft, childlike voice. Monster-X can disappear instantly and has never been seen by an adult. Everything we know about this monster is based on eye-witness accounts from children. Its similarity to a Tyrannosaurus rex has led some monstrologists to disregard it as pure fantasy, but until I see firm proof of its nonexistence, I will regard it as a real creature. A compelling body of evidence speaks to its existence (see below).
LIFE CYCLE	Like other reptiles, Monster-X lays eggs. Mysterious, multicolored eggshells (see fig. 1) have been found in backyards and parks, especially in the month of April, and they are believed to have contained Monster-X babies. The egg-laying season for Monster-X appears to coincide with Easter egg hunts. Some eyewitness reports might be tainted by the hyperactive imaginations of children who have eaten lots of candy.
SAFETY MEASURES	Not applicable.

ACCORDING TO THE EYE-WITNESS ACCOUNT OF JAMES WAGNER, AGE 9, DURING A FAMILY VACATION IN ORLANDO, FLORIDA, THIS MONSTER STOLE HIS SISTER'S CANDY. JAMES SWEARS HE DIDN'T DO IT.

Northern Boulder Beast

DANGER TO HUMANS

This is how the Boulder Beast hides, often in full view but in perfect camouflage.

LATIN NAME	*Monstrum saxitille boreale*
HABITAT	The Northern Boulder Beast lives in forests and meadows near human dwellings in the Northern Hemisphere. The monster is often encountered in shallow caves or holes in the ground.
DIET	These beasts eat nuts, berries, children, and pets.
DISTINGUISHING FEATURES	The Boulder Beast is dumb and can be easily fooled. If you pretend to throw it a nut, the throwing motion will cause the Beast to spend hours looking for it. But the Boulder Beast is also a very patient hunter and forager. It feeds only a few times a month and can remain in a motionless, hibernating state between feedings, during which times it can be mistaken for a large boulder or rock. This ability also allows it to surprise unsuspecting prey. Once you have been caught by a Boulder Beast, you stand little chance of breaking free from its mighty grip. Boulder Beasts can reach 7 feet in height (if they were to stand up straight) and can weigh up to 600 pounds.

LIFE CYCLE	Boulder Beasts can live for more than 250 years and are known to take good care of their offspring. In its early hundreds a Beast forms a strong relationship with a male or female and then stays with its mate for life. A baby Boulder Beast lives with its mother and father, who share parental duties equally, for 60 to 80 years. Even after it reaches maturity, it often hangs around its parents' hunting grounds. The Beast's development is a slow one, and you could compare a 100-year-old Boulder Beast to an 18- to 20-year-old human. Many Boulder Beasts don't move away from their parents until they are well over 100 years old.
SAFETY MEASURES	The Boulder Beast gives off a strong odor of sulfur—in short, it stinks like rotten eggs, making it easy to detect. If you get a whiff of this creature, be wary of where you are walking.

Copy of Aooga tribal art, Aooga Island, Dec. 1947

"The Monster"

THIS DRAWING SHOWS WHAT IS BELIEVED TO BE THE SOUTHERN BOULDER BEAST. ITS APPEARANCE AND HABITS ARE SIMILAR TO THOSE OF THE NORTHERN VARIETY, BUT IT IS SAID TO GIVE OFF A RATHER PLEASANT SMELL OF COCONUT.

I OBSERVED THIS MOTHER BOULDER BEAST AND HER CHILD FOR SEVERAL MINUTES WHEN I LEFT A BACKYARD BARBEQUE TO INVESTIGATE A SUSPICIOUS SMELL. I ESTIMATE THIS CHILD TO BE 40 YEARS OLD.

BOULDER BEAST
Mother & baby

TARA'S BACKYARD MEMORIAL DAY 2004

PATOOTY

LATIN NAME	*Raptor deliciarum*
HABITAT	The Patooty lives in children's bedrooms, often nesting in closets or under beds.
DIET	The Patooty eats plush toys.
DISTINGUISHING FEATURES	This monster is not as cute as its name and appearance suggest. In fact, the Patooty is a nasty little critter that torments children and can be quite a bully once it moves into a child's room. After an initial period during which the monster makes friends with the child, the Patooty turns threatening. It can't stand other cute things and will start eating toys. At first one or two go missing, but eventually it will devour every toy in the room.

The Patooty doesn't speak any known language but gurgles like a baby and growls and grunts to communicate.

The Patooty has retractable claws of phenomenal sharpness and a very strong bite. It grows to the size of a large teddy bear and can weigh up to 20 pounds.

LIFE CYCLE	Patooties appear out of nowhere when fully grown and disappear when they have eaten all the toys in a child's room.
SAFETY MEASURES	Hide your teddy bears and other toys.

I OBSERVED THIS PATOOTY TEARING INTO A TEDDY BEAR AFTER A LONG STAKEOUT AT THE HOUSE OF 6-YEAR-OLD JAMAL IN NEW YORK CITY.

The Patooty

THIS IS A PIECE OF A BOOK JACKET I FOUND IN AN ANTIQUE STORE IN MASSACHUSETTS. THE BOOK TO WHICH IT BELONGED WAS MISSING.

A CLOSE-UP OF THE PATOOTY'S EXTREMELY SHARP, RETRACTABLE CLAWS. THE CLAWS ARE ITS PRIMARY WEAPON, USED TO DESTROY TOYS AND TO THREATEN CHILDREN.

RAZOR-TWIGGED
TREE BEAST

DANGER TO HUMANS

LATIN NAME	*Bestia virganovaculata*
HABITAT	This monster lives in trees, especially older ones that grow close to houses.
DIET	The Razor-Twigged Tree Beast consumes only liquids. It prefers syrup and blood but will accept any thick, sweet, or savory fluid.
DISTINGUISHING FEATURES	During windy nights the Tree Beast's long, slender body reaches toward windows, and its razor-sharp "fingers" scratch the windowpanes until they break. Once in the presence of prey, it punctures the surface to release blood or syrup, then absorbs the liquid through its rootlike feet. The Tree Beast is only active during the dark nights of fall and early winter. It can grow up to 4 feet in length and weigh as much as a pound.

LIFE CYCLE	Tree Beasts grow out of lumps that form on older tree trunks. The monsters grow up as young, healthy-looking twigs, drawing their energy from the tree sap. As they mature, they begin to migrate toward the branches of trees that hang close to homes. They live for one year and will look like any other dead branch when they fall to the ground between March and April.
SAFETY MEASURES	Don't sleep near the window.

THIS ANCIENT APPLE TREE STANDS NEXT TO A SMALL COTTAGE IN NORTHERN GERMANY. IT IS ALLEGED TO HAVE PRODUCED MANY GENERATIONS OF TREE BEASTS. PEOPLE REFUSE TO EAT THE APPLES, WHICH SOME BELIEVE HAVE MAGICAL POWERS AND OTHERS SAY ARE POISONOUS.

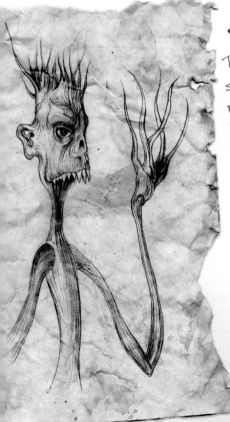

THIS UNDATED, UNSIGNED DRAWING SHOWS A PARTICULARLY FRIGHTENING-LOOKING TREE BEAST. IT IS THE MOST DETAILED DEPICTION OF A RAZOR-TWIGGED TREE BEAST IN EXISTENCE. THE ARTIST MUST HAVE HAD AMPLE TIME TO OBSERVE IT, PERHAPS WHILE HOLDING THE MONSTER IN CAPTIVITY—AN INCREDIBLY DIFFICULT TASK, SINCE THE BEAST'S FINGERS CAN CUT ALMOST ANY MATERIAL.

TREE BEASTS GROW OUT OF THE GNARLY LUMPS YOU OFTEN FIND ON OLD TREES.

Shadow-Caster

LATIN NAME	*Umbrator tremendus*
HABITAT	Shadow-Casters live indoors, especially in dark corners, in closets, and under beds and other furniture.
DIET	These monsters eat human nail clippings and hair.
DISTINGUISHING FEATURES	The Shadow-Caster lurks in the dark areas of rooms until given an opportunity to cast its signature shadow by placing itself in front of a light source. It is believed that this behavior serves to frighten humans, causing them to release excess hair due to stress, thus producing food for the Caster.

An adult Shadow-Caster is less than a foot tall and weighs less than a pound.

Large, fully grown Casters sometimes attack sleeping children, nibbling at their toes and fingernails.

The Shadow-Caster makes a sound that resembles creaking floorboards. |

LIFE CYCLE	The Shadow-Caster lives with its family. Baby Casters, or Chicks, stay with the father most of the time, while the mother hunts for food. You can sometimes see female Casters carrying big bundles of hair back to their lair.
SAFETY MEASURES	When sleeping, keep your feet (and head, if possible) under the covers.

A FATHER AND HIS CHICKS.

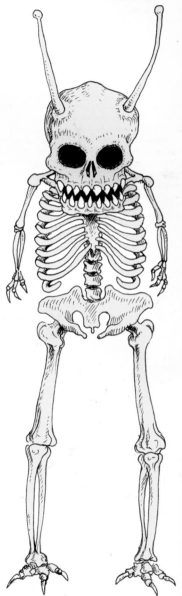

THE CASTER IS RARELY SEEN UP CLOSE. I CAUGHT THIS ONE TRYING TO BITE MY PINKY NAIL WHEN I WAS 12 YEARS OLD. I PUT AN EMPTY GLASS JAR OVER IT TO HOLD IT CAPTIVE UNTIL THE MORNING, BUT IT ESCAPED. I HAD TO SLEEP WITH SHOES, A HAT, AND GLOVES ON FOR WEEKS AFTER THAT, AS CASTERS ARE VENGEFUL CREATURES.

THIS DRAWING SHOWS THE SHADOW-CASTER'S SKELETON. IT IS HARD TO PICTURE THE SHAPE WHEN OBSERVING A LIVE CASTER, SINCE ITS FUR IS SO THICK AND FLUFFY.

SLOBBER BUG

DANGER TO HUMANS

LATIN NAME	*Cimex salivans*
HABITAT	This monster dwells under beds and sinks, behind washing machines, and in other hiding places around the house.
DIET	The Slobber Bug is not a picky eater. It devours absolutely everything: meat, vegetables, plastics, fabrics, and metal. Favorite meals include socks and other dirty laundry.

DISTINGUISHING FEATURES	The Slobber Bug's most fascinating feature is its unusual digestion technique: it drenches food in its corrosive saliva before slurping up the half-digested food with its big tongue and scarfing it down with a loud *smack*.
	
	    The Bug expands its large, spongy backside by almost 100 percent in order to hold more food. It can grow to about 5 feet in length and weigh more than 100 pounds when filled to capacity.
	
	    The Slobber Bug can cause severe injury to humans with its saliva, though it does not actively hunt people (despite a German report about a child who fell asleep in a pile of dirty laundry).

LIFE CYCLE	The Bug's life cycle is similar to that of many insects: the monster begins life as a larva and reaches its mature stage after transforming within a cocoon. These cocoons are usually found attached to wood or concrete in attics and basements and are about the size of a football.
SAFETY MEASURES	The Slobber Bug hates cats, so purchasing a feline ensures that a Slobber Bug will make a swift departure from your home.

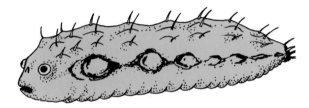

THE SLOBBER BUG LARVA DOES NOT HAVE CORROSIVE SALIVA YET; IT EATS LINT AND DUST.

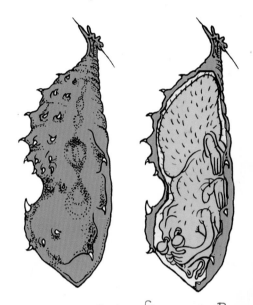

THE COCOON OF THE SLOBBER BUG IS COVERED WITH THORNS. IN THE CUT-AWAY IMAGE TO THE RIGHT, YOU CAN SEE THE BUG TRANSFORMING INTO ITS ADULT BODY.

THIS STONE SCULPTURE OF A PRE-COLOMBIAN DEITY WAS FOUND NEAR TEGUCIGALPA, HONDURAS. THE GOD WAS SAID TO HAVE THE POWER TO DEVOUR THE WORLD. TO ME, IT SOUNDS AND LOOKS LIKE THE SLOBBER BUG.

SNOUTED GRABBER

LATIN NAME	*Ereptor rostratus*
HABITAT	Snouted Grabbers live anywhere in a house where they can find storage space and some quiet, often in the corners of attics or basements.
DIET	The Grabber is a skimmer—it eats the end pieces of loaves of bread, the slightly damaged apple that has been left out for too long, and other leftovers from human meals.
DISTINGUISHING FEATURES	As the name implies, this monster seizes any opportunity to grab things. It is a hoarder of stuff. Anything that's not screwed down might attract a Grabber, and you'll end up finding piles of lost items in the Grabber's nesting area in some remote part of your house. Grabbers grow to be 4 feet tall and weigh approximately 45 pounds. The Grabber's body is malleable, and like a mouse or a rat, it can squeeze through passages that appear much too small for it.

THIS IS MY FRIEND WOLFGANG'S BASEMENT, NEXT TO THE WATER HEATER. IT IS A DIRTY AND SMELLY AREA FULL OF ALL KINDS OF JUNK. (IT'S HARD TO TELL WHICH PART IS WOLFGANG'S DOING AND WHICH PART IS THE GRABBER'S, WHO NESTED THERE, AS WOLFGANG IS QUITE MESSY AND NEVER THROWS ANYTHING AWAY.)

LIFE CYCLE	It is common to find footprints and bite marks from young Snouted Grabbers in or around their nests, but the young monsters themselves have never been seen. Many believe that baby Grabbers are invisible, and some monstrologists even suggest that the adult Grabber retains the capacity to become invisible at will.
SAFETY MEASURES	Not applicable, though spring cleaning is said to inhibit the Grabber.

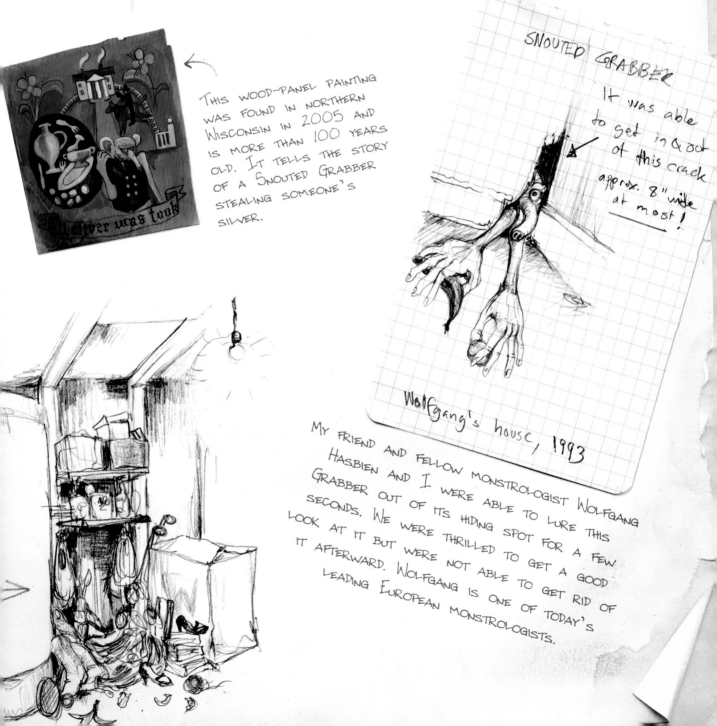

THIS WOOD-PANEL PAINTING WAS FOUND IN NORTHERN WISCONSIN IN 2005 AND IS MORE THAN 100 YEARS OLD. IT TELLS THE STORY OF A SNOUTED GRABBER STEALING SOMEONE'S SILVER.

SNOUTED GRABBER

It was able to get in & out of this crack approx. 8" wide at most!

Wolfgang's house, 1993

MY FRIEND AND FELLOW MONSTROLOGIST WOLFGANG HASBIEN AND I WERE ABLE TO LURE THIS GRABBER OUT OF ITS HIDING SPOT FOR A FEW SECONDS. WE WERE THRILLED TO GET A GOOD LOOK AT IT BUT WERE NOT ABLE TO GET RID OF IT AFTERWARD. WOLFGANG IS ONE OF TODAY'S LEADING EUROPEAN MONSTROLOGISTS.

TADPOLE-MONSTER

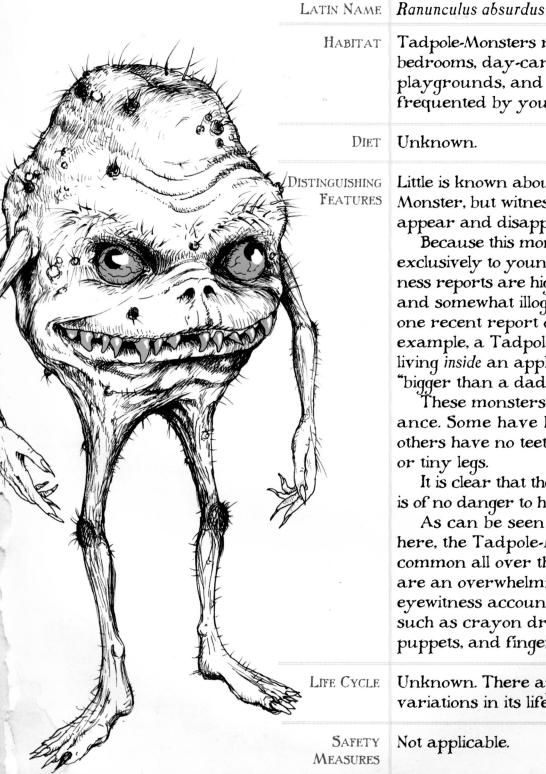

LATIN NAME	*Ranunculus absurdus*
HABITAT	Tadpole-Monsters reside in bedrooms, day-care centers, playgrounds, and other areas frequented by young children.
DIET	Unknown.

DISTINGUISHING FEATURES	Little is known about the Tadpole-Monster, but witnesses say it can appear and disappear in an instant.
	    Because this monster shows itself exclusively to young children, the witness reports are highly incoherent and somewhat illogical. According to one recent report of a sighting, for example, a Tadpole-Monster was living *inside* an apple, while also being "bigger than a daddy."
	    These monsters vary in appearance. Some have big fangs, while others have no teeth but huge hands or tiny legs.
	    It is clear that the Tadpole-Monster is of no danger to humans.
	    As can be seen from the images here, the Tadpole-Monster is common all over the world. There are an overwhelming number of eyewitness accounts and depictions, such as crayon drawings, paper puppets, and finger paintings.

LIFE CYCLE	Unknown. There appear to be great variations in its life cycle.
SAFETY MEASURES	Not applicable.

A TYPICAL EYEWITNESS DRAWING. THIS ONE COMES FROM GLEN KOZAK, A FOUR-AND-A-HALF YEAR OLD LIVING IN ANCHORAGE, ALASKA. HE DESCRIBED THE MONSTER AS "NICE."

THIS DRAWING WAS MADE WITH A BLACK MARKER AND WAS DRAWN ABOUT 2 FEET ABOVE THE GROUND AT LUCKY BELLS DAY-CARE CENTER IN TUSCALOOSA, ALABAMA. IT WAS FOUND IN 2007. IT IS A GOOD EXAMPLE OF THE VARIATIONS THAT OCCUR WITHIN THIS SPECIES.

Fig. 29
1/20

THESE PETROGLYPHS, OR ROCK DRAWINGS, FOUND IN SOUTH-WESTERN SWEDEN SHOW ANIMALS AND PEOPLE RUNNING FROM A TADPOLE-MONSTER AND WERE MADE 10,000 TO 15,000 YEARS AGO.

Toe-Eater

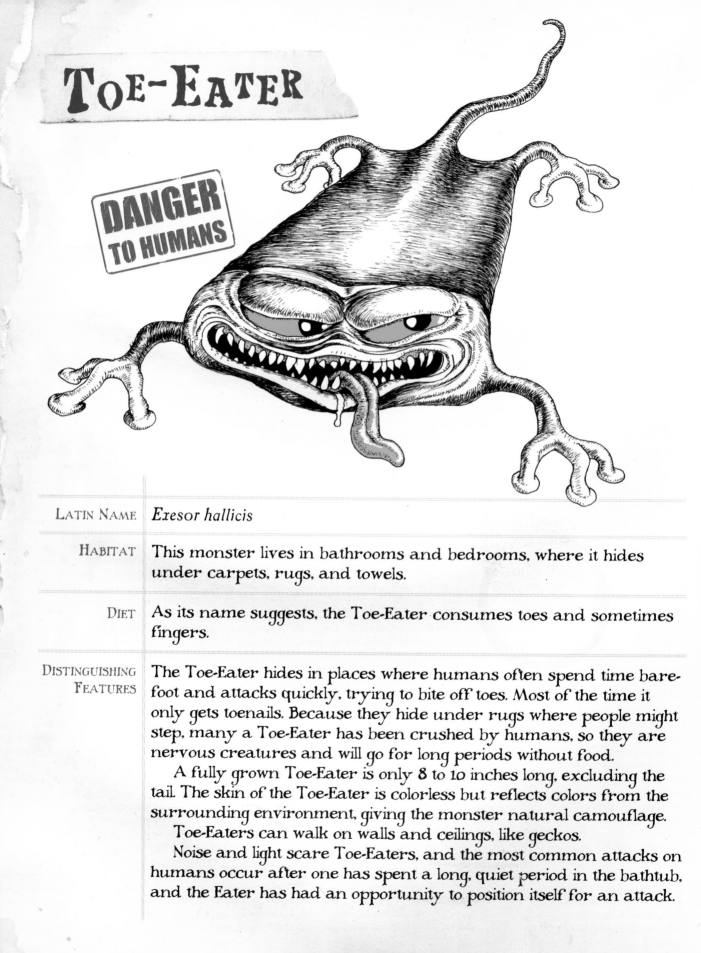

DANGER TO HUMANS

LATIN NAME	*Exesor hallicis*
HABITAT	This monster lives in bathrooms and bedrooms, where it hides under carpets, rugs, and towels.
DIET	As its name suggests, the Toe-Eater consumes toes and sometimes fingers.
DISTINGUISHING FEATURES	The Toe-Eater hides in places where humans often spend time barefoot and attacks quickly, trying to bite off toes. Most of the time it only gets toenails. Because they hide under rugs where people might step, many a Toe-Eater has been crushed by humans, so they are nervous creatures and will go for long periods without food.

A fully grown Toe-Eater is only 8 to 10 inches long, excluding the tail. The skin of the Toe-Eater is colorless but reflects colors from the surrounding environment, giving the monster natural camouflage.

Toe-Eaters can walk on walls and ceilings, like geckos.

Noise and light scare Toe-Eaters, and the most common attacks on humans occur after one has spent a long, quiet period in the bathtub, and the Eater has had an opportunity to position itself for an attack.

LIFE CYCLE	The Toe-Eater is assumed to live a short and dangerous life. It lays eggs, often in toilet tanks, and then leaves. Baby Toe-Eaters, called Nibblers, must fend for themselves.
SAFETY MEASURES	Don't take extra long baths. Always put on the light in the bathroom, and try to make noise when you're relaxing in the tub. I like to sing when I take a bath, and that keeps the Toe-Eaters away.

I WAS CALLED IN TO INVESTIGATE A POSSIBLE TOE-EATER SITUATION IN A PRIVATE RESIDENCE IN TACOMA, WASHINGTON. I FOUND THIS TOE-EATER HIDING UNDER THE BATHROOM RUG, READY TO POUNCE.

7-12-04

THESE ARE TYPICAL TOE-EATER EGGS. THEY RESEMBLE SMALL PIECES OF USED SOAP.

ONE TOE-EATER SAT THERE FOR 30 MIN. WAITING FOR PREY. ← NEXT PAGE

WE SAW IT ONCE MORE, BUT THIS TIME IT CHOSE AN UNFORTUNATE LOCATION: IT CREPT ALONG THE WALL ABOVE THE TOILET AND THEN FELL IN ACCIDENTALLY. I FLUSHED IT DOWN QUICKLY, AND THE PROBLEM WAS SOLVED.

THE SAME TOE-EATER ON THE WALL BY SHOWER

TWO-TOED JUMPING RAT

LATIN NAME	*Rattus subsultans*
HABITAT	Two-Toed Jumping Rats live in dark, moist, indoor areas, such as basements, garages, and laundry rooms.
DIET	This monster is omnivorous: It eats anything it can get its paws on, from kitchen leftovers to motor oil.
DISTINGUISHING FEATURES	Curious and nosy, the Two-Toed Jumping Rat sneaks around the house looking for food.

This monster is harmless to humans but can give off a repulsive odor if it feels threatened. The stench can be extremely hard to remove, similar to that of skunk spray. Washing with tomato juice is said to help.

The biggest Jumping Rat ever reported was approximately 6 feet tall, but the more common size is between 3 and 4 feet.

Its powerful hind legs give it the ability to jump high and travel long distances.

THIS CLOSE-UP VIEW OF A JUMPING RAT SHOWS ITS ROGUISH FACIAL EXPRESSION.

LIFE CYCLE	The Jumping Rat has dozens of babies at a time. The baby Rats are left without any care and often become a serious nuisance, as they devour items all over a house. You might, for instance, find them gnawing on metal pipes and drywall. They seem to be impervious to electricity and will gladly eat live electrical wires, slurping them up like strands of spaghetti, with sparks flying.
SAFETY MEASURES	Keeping a tidy house makes it harder for the Jumping Rat to find food.

NOT ONLY ARE THE FOOTPRINTS OF THE TWO-TOED JUMPING RAT DISTINCT BECAUSE OF THE SHAPE OF THEIR FEET, BUT EACH PAIR OF PRINTS IS ALSO PLACED UNUSUALLY FAR APART. YOU WILL SEE ONE PAIR OF FOOTPRINTS AT ONE LOCATION, AND THE NEXT SET WILL BE ANYWHERE FROM A FEW FEET TO AS MANY AS 20 FEET AWAY, MAKING IT A VERY DIFFICULT MONSTER TO TRACK.

Rattus Gigant

THE TWO-TOED JUMPING RAT ORIGINATED IN NORTH AMERICA. THIS ILLUSTRATION COMES FROM A BOOK BY THE LITTLE-KNOWN 16TH-CENTURY EXPLORER UMBERTO DE LIRIOUS THAT DETAILS HIS TRAVELS IN THE NEW WORLD. ON PAGE 53 OF HIS BOOK, HE DESCRIBES A BRIEF ENCOUNTER WITH A MONSTER RESEMBLING THE JUMPING RAT. HE NAMED IT "GIANT RAT" IN LATIN. IN DE LIRIOUS'S ACCOUNT, THE RAT EATS MOST OF HIS SOLDIERS' GUNPOWDER, PUTTING THE WHOLE EXPEDITION AT RISK.

WEARM

DANGER
TO HUMANS

LATIN NAME	*Vermis auris*
HABITAT	The Wearm lives inside humans.
DIET	Humans.
DISTINGUISHING FEATURES	Thankfully, this is a rare monster.

When the Wearm is about the size of a slug, it infiltrates humans through their ears. It wiggles in through the ear canal—the more squishy earwax there is, the quicker the invasion—then enters the brain stem and starts eating and growing at a slow pace. Eventually, the Wearm consumes its host from within.

It is, in other words, one of the most gruesome monsters known to humankind. However, the process of consuming the host is slow, and a Wearm doesn't really become a threat until it is 75 to 80 years old. Before that, you might be a host and not even know it.

LIFE CYCLE	Wearms lay microscopic eggs that travel through the host's digestive tract. Once they are excreted by the human digestive system, sewers might take them anywhere.
	After hatching, the young Wearms spend the early part of their lives looking for a human host. During this time, many of them get eaten by birds.
SAFETY MEASURES	In order to keep yourself safe from Wearms, ear hygiene is encouraged, since the Wearm appears to be attracted to people with excessive amounts of earwax.

BRANCH

THE WEARM'S SMALL TENTACLES
GROW INTO ELABORATE BRANCHES
THAT CONNECT WITH THE HUMAN
NERVOUS SYSTEM, WHICH WEARMS
USE AS THEIR ENERGY SOURCE.

TENTACLE

1mm

WEARM

Feb. 27 - 98

WEARM EGGS LOOK
LIKE SMALL SEEDS
THROUGH THE LENS OF
A MICROSCOPE.

I CAUGHT THIS WEARM IN SAN DIEGO, CALIFORNIA, IN
1998. A CLIENT SUSPECTED THAT A WEARM HAD INFECTED
HIS GRANDFATHER, WHO WAS 96 AND HAD VERY WAXY
EARS. HE CALLED ME JUST IN TIME: THIS YOUNG WEARM
WAS ABOUT TO ENTER MY CLIENT'S EAR, AND I LATER
ERADICATED 4 MORE WEARMS AROUND THE HOUSE.